P9-BTN-737

3 5674 04625979 3

This book belongs to:

578-8002

DETROIT, MI 48235

17731 W. SEVEN MILE RD.

BRANCH LIBRARY

CHASE BRANCH LIBRARY
17731 W. SEVEN MILE RD.
DETROIT, MI 48235
578-8002

OCT 2007

CH

Rob M. Worley
&
Mike Dubisch

When adventure is your destination!

Boston • Detroit • New York • Phoenix

Visit us online at www.actionopolis.com

ACTIONOPOLIS
Published by Komikwerks, LLC
1 Ruth Street Worcester, MA 01602

KOMIKWERKS

Heir to Fire: Gila Flats, Copyright © 2006 by Actionopolis, LLC • All right reserved, including the right of reproduction in whole or in part in any form • ACTIONOPOLIS and the Actionopolis logo are copyright © 2006 Actionopolis, LLC • KOMIKWERKS and the Komikwerks logo are copyright © 2006 Komikwerks, LLC.

Created by Actionopolis, Rob M. Worley and Mike Dubisch
Based on a concept by Shannon Eric Denton and Patrick Coyle

First Edition

Printed in China.

DISTRIBUTED BY PUBLISHERS GROUP WEST

This novel is a work of fiction. Names, characters, places, and incidents are either the product of the author's imagination, or if real, used fictitiously. Any resemblance to persons living or dead is strictly coincidental.

Library of Congress Cataloging-in-Publication Data
Worley, Rob
Heir to Fire: Gila Flats / Rob M. Worley and Mike Dubsich
p. cm. – (Heir to Fire: Gila Flats ; 1)
Summary: When monstrous creatures overtake Ryan Morales' hometown, he must set aside his fears and unleash the secret power that burns within him.
ISBN: 0-9742803-7-2
[1. Legends–Juvenile Fiction. 2. Friendship–Juvenile Fiction.]
I. Dubisch, Mike II. Title
2006902384

Other books from

• The Anubis Tapestry •

• Blackfoot Braves Society •

• The Forest King •

• Spirit of the Samurai •

• What I Did On My Hypergalactic
Interstellar Summer Vacation •

And more coming soon!

For more information on
Heir to Fire or any of our other
exciting books, visit our website:
www.actionopolis.com

Table of Contents

Prologue i

Chapter One:
Things get hot on Main Street 1

Chapter Two:
Ryan returns home 9

Chapter Three:
Discoveries, strange and frightening 17

Chapter Four:
Things cool off and then boil over 27

Chapter Five:
The word and the crater 37

Chapter Six:
Things change for Donut and Ryan **45**

Chapter Seven:
Akashalon **59**

Chapter Eight:
Brain Stingers **67**

Chapter Nine:
The Fire Prince **79**

Chapter Ten:
"Behold...the Mygantuan!" **89**

Chapter Eleven:
Battle for Main Street **105**

Epilogue **126**

List of Full-Page Illustrations

"I'm spinnin' gold here, and you're not even listening." . . v

Kirby 8

Donut's second favorite activity. 16

Their unwavering stare 26

It looked like the road had just collapsed into an
underground cave. 36

"That's troubling." 44

The sphere glowed yellow and pulsed like a tiny sun. . . . 58

Akashalon! 62

"Don't be afraid, Ryan." 66

"I'm no hero." 78

The whole town was slowly shuffling toward them . . 88

"Behold...the Mygantuan!" 102

"...Always familiars of the Firekind..." 104

Ryan rode atop the giant lizard. 114

He was engulfed in a sheath of hot, red flame . . . 122

To my parents,
Jerry and Kathie,
who lit the fire.
—Rob

To Jade, and
to the long night.
—Mike

Prologue

Mrs. Thelma Peters checked her watch for third time in two minutes.

"Your time's just about up," she muttered in a quiet, impatient voice as she strained to read the numbers in the dim light of the empty ranch house.

She reached into the pocket of her blazer and produced the puzzling note that had brought her here. The first strange thing was that the note was hand-written. Thelma had come to believe that hand-written notes were a dead art form. But even stranger was that at some time

i

the night before someone had slipped this request under her office door:

"Wish to acquire the Oobakka estate. Willing to pay highest price. Meet me there at 7 a.m. today."

Thelma's watch told her it was now 7:30, and there was no sign of the mysterious, would-be homebuyer. She had searched through the house but found no one, and was now back in the two-story great room. No realtor had ever been able to sell the house. It had a reputation in the town of having once been the scene of a horrible tragedy.

"Looks like I won't be selling you today, you terrible, terrible place," Thelma said out loud. She laughed at herself, talking to the house as if the stories about it were true. "Enough of this. I've got places to be…houses to sell."

Thelma turned for the front door, only to feel the strangest and most unnerving sensation she'd ever experienced. It felt as if were lying facedown in a hammock of stretched canvas, except she was standing upright. She saw nothing in front of her, but felt something pressing against her body, her legs, and even tickling her face.

Thelma instinctively tried to brush whatever it was away, but found that she couldn't move her arms. They were held firm by this strange force.

The morning sunlight showed through the moth-eaten blinds, illuminating the barrier…a strange weave of silken threads, some of which floated in the air like pipe smoke. The threads didn't look strong enough to support anything more than a button from her realtor's coat, yet they held her snug and completely immobile.

The sunlight also revealed something else, a large dark shape moving down the wall of the great room like an inky shadow, spreading out from a crevice and heading directly toward Mrs. Peters.

Her heart pounding in her chest, Thelma watched as

it flowed from the wall to the barrier she was ensnared on, edging closer to her face. As it approached, she realized that this was not one shape, but hundreds of tiny shapes moving as one.

And Thelma Peters was too terrified to even scream...

"I'm spinnin' gold here, and you're not even listening."

Chapter One

Things Get Hot On Main Street

"The thing to remember about gals is, they're more scared of you then y'all are of them," Albert croaked as he dug into the hard packed ice cream with his stainless steel scoop. His slow, confident drawl always made Ryan think of cowboys.

Albert's deeply tanned face was as cracked and craggy as the dry desert that surrounded their tiny town of Gila Flats. With his bushy grey eyebrows, thick mustache, and white stubble on his cheeks, he did indeed look like he'd be better suited to riding the open range on horseback than dropping scoops into cones behind the ice cream counter.

1

"Now you're about to ask me again if'n I'm a cowboy. Ain'cha?"

The old man grinned a big toothy grin as Ryan's cheeks flushed hot red. He had asked Albert that question once, the first time his folks took him to the ice cream parlor. That had been nine years ago, when Ryan was just five. Much as he liked Albert, he hated it when he brought up the cowboy thing. It made him feel like a stupid little kid again.

He was fourteen now, and not so little. He was going through what all the adults called a "growth spurt." He was taller than his mom, and they said soon he'd be taller than his dad. He was already taller than most kids in his school.

Ryan stole a glance out the shop's front window. Across the street, Corrine Babbot sat with Dawn Haughey on the bench outside Thompkin's Hardware store, waiting for her folks to pick her up. Ryan always thought that if he grew taller he would have more confidence, but one look at Corrine made him want to bolt out the back door.

"Ryan, have you heard one word I said to you?" Albert asked, shaking his head in disbelief. "Don't go gettin' all flustered 'fore you even talk to her. I'm spinning gold here, and you're not even listening. I'm an expert on the fair ones."

"Fair ones" was Albert's favorite word for "girls."

"Is that on account of you being married five times?" Ryan asked, smiling and getting his composure back.

"Now don't sass me, whipper-snapper," Albert said, handing Ryan two waffle cones filled enormous scoops of ice cream, one chocolate, one vanilla. "Here I am, tryin' to help a fella out with some sagely words and cold treats, and all I get is sass."

Ryan smirked out a quiet laugh. "Sorry, Albert."

"Now you just take these treats over to the fair ones, say 'hello' real polite, and tell her your name. If one thing don't lead to another, I'll refund half the difference."

Ryan backed into the glass door and pushed it open, letting a gust of hot, dry air into the cool store. "I have no idea what that means."

"You just be yourself. Hear?"

"Great. Never heard that one before," Ryan said, letting the door close behind him.

With each step, he felt the strength leaving his legs as he struggled across the hot blacktop to where Corrine and Dawn sat chatting. He gulped, but the inside of his throat was sticky and dry, and a sudden wave of panic washed over him as he realized that when he reached the bench he probably wouldn't be able to speak. For sure his voice would crack. That was a given.

Ryan drew a deep breath and forced himself to continue. His vision seemed to cloud with dark dots, and the street seemed as if it was tilting like the deck of a sinking ship. He felt like he was stumbling around, awkward as a baby bird, gripping the waffle cones, which had grown soft and squishy in his hands. But if he truly was staggering, the girls took no notice of him at all.

Finally he was there, standing right in front of

Corrine, vanilla dripping down his right hand and chocolate over his left. The bright Arizona sun seemed to reflect a blinding halo off of Corrine's shiny blond hair. She looked

up at him, squinted and smiled.

"Hi, Ryan," she said and his panic intensified.

I was supposed to tell her my name, Ryan's thoughts raced through his head. *She already knows my name. What do I say now?* The best he could come up was, "Here," as he clumsily thrust the ice cream cones at the two girls.

Corrine leaped off the bench, but Dawn was a sitting

duck as liquefied chocolate and vanilla ice cream splashed over her hair, face, shirt, and book bag. Ryan stared in slack-jawed amazement. The ice cream had completely melted in the time it took him to cross the street.

"You idiot," Dawn raged even as Corrine tried to stifle giggles.

"It's just ice cream," Corrine said, swiping Dawn's arm with her finger, taking a bit of chocolate for herself.

Ryan dug his sticky hands into his pockets and pulled out fistfuls of napkins from the ice cream shop. "Must have melted," he mumbled and offered the paper towels, which Dawn angrily snatched from him. She said something pointed, but Ryan couldn't hear her. He was lost in a wave of humiliation.

Behind Ryan, a shiny new SUV pulled up to the curb and both girls went over to it. It belonged to Corrine's father. Mortified, Ryan stood frozen as they got in. The girls were still talking, but he turned around, feeling like he was miles away. Then he heard Corrine say, "but he's cute. I want to ask him."

And then: "Hey, Ryan."

Ryan turned and looked at Corrine's smile. "We're having people over to the pool on Saturday. Want to come?"

Ryan couldn't help but smile back at her. "Sure."

"Cool blue. Bring a friend if you want."

And then she was back in the car and gone.

Kirby

Chapter Two

Ryan Returns Home

Ryan walked along a picket fence that surrounded the dusty tract of land that Mrs. Wilkensen called her front yard, but he may as well have been walking on the moon. His head was still dizzy from his conversation with Corrine and the invitation to her pool party.

A dark shape leaped towards Ryan, issuing a short, sharp, high-pitched noise that startled him from his blissful daydream and sent him jumping two feet in the air. The sound wasn't really that frightening. Ryan just hadn't expected to hear his cat's loud greeting as it jumped up on the picket fence in hopes of walking alongside him, shoulder to shoulder.

9

"You scared me, Kirby." Ryan laughed as he snatched the red tabby off the fence and carried him the rest of the way. He wasn't the only one who had heard the cat. Old Mrs. Wilkensen hobbled out on her front porch like a wicked witch appearing in a cloud of black smoke.

"You get that cat away from my house," she yelled. Ryan was amazed she had heard Kirby's little yelp. Her ears functioned like huge radar dishes, waiting for a reason to pop out of her house and start screaming at anyone passing by. "I've told you a million times! I hate cats! They make a foul odor and I'm allergic and I resent them being in my yard!"

"He's not in your yard," Ryan said, smiling cordially as he picked up the pace. Technically, it was true. Kirby was, in fact, no longer in the yard as he crossed the property line to his own house. "See ya, Mrs. Wilkensen."

A sound like a tiny motorcycle engine purred from Kirby's muzzle as Ryan bounded up the stone steps to his family's porch and opened the heavy door leading into his home.

Inside he was greeted with a gust of cold air. He dropped Kirby, who charged through the house like a tiger before finding his prey: a bowl of cat kibble in the kitchen.

"Close the door," Ryan's mother, Rose Morales, said. "It's ninety-eight degrees out there."

"I love you too, mom," Ryan replied, and closed the door, which promptly bounced open again. The door had a tricky deadbolt on it, which had a habit of sliding when the door was open, but was stubborn about locking when the door was closed. Rose was constantly asking Ryan's father to fix it, but he was a busy man.

"I'm sorry, dear, but we're just trying to keep the house cool. Your father spent the whole day sweating in the desert."

Ryan shivered as his mother went back into the kitchen and continued preparing dinner. As soon as she was out of sight, the boy checked the thermostat. It read seventy-five degrees, but Ryan already had goose bumps. He nudged it up to seventy-eight and sat down on the couch as his father entered the living room.

"They say it'll break one hundred tomorrow," said Rick Morales, still wearing his sweat-soaked border patrol uniform. He checked the thermostat and turned it down to seventy-four. "How was school, son?" he asked as they both sat down at the kitchen table, with Ryan's Mom placing a plate of meat loaf and a bowl of salad in front of them.

"Great," Ryan exclaimed, not realizing he was grinning as wide as the horizon.

His parents froze like statues and looked at each other gravely. Ryan's smile faded a bit as they both slowly turned to him, their eyes squinting into narrow slits of mistrust.

"What have you done with our son?" Mom asked in mock accusation.

"Our Ryan doesn't say school is 'Great.' Our Ryan hates school!" Dad said in a low, somber voice.

"This Ryan is a fake!" Mom broke character and giggled.

"Shut up," Ryan said, laughing with them. "I meant after school. After school was great. I got invited to a pool party on Saturday."

"Really? Who invited you?" Mom asked.

"A friend," said Ryan, squirming. This was going to get embarrassing. Because he was shy, Ryan didn't make a lot of friends. Which meant his mother made too big a deal out of any new people he met. And this was the worst case: a friend who is a girl. Suffering through Mom's excitement could be excruciating.

"A friend? Does this friend have a name?"

Ryan decided it was best to just bite the bullet and get it over with. "Corrine invited me."

His mother brightened at the name. Ryan never had a girlfriend before, and she knew that Ryan liked Corrine. "Corrine," Mom said effusively.

"Rose," Rick cautioned his wife. Ryan was sure his dad could feel the heat coming off his red cheeks.

She inhaled a deep breath, exhaled slowly, and placed her hands palms-down on the table, struggling to mask her enthusiasm over her son's burgeoning social life. "We shall never speak of it again," she said, holding back a smile. "You can discuss the details with your father, who shall transport you to the event."

Ryan's embarrassment faded in light of his mother's acting, and he snorted with laughter. "Thanks, Mom. I'm gonna go ask Donut if he wants to go with."

Ryan jumped up from the table and headed for the door. "Ryan," Dad protested. "Your mother made dinner for us to-"

Rose put a hand on Rick's arm, interrupting him from stopping his son. "Let him go. Look how excited he is."

"See ya, Dad! See ya, Mom," Ryan yelled as he closed the door behind him.

* * *

"Sometimes I'd wondered if he'd ever fit in," Rose

confided in Rick after her son left the house.

"I always said everything would be all right, didn't I?" Rick replied. "Sometimes I still wonder where that boy came from that makes him so different from everyone else. Maybe it's time."

"No," Rose said with a frown. "It's not time yet."

"He needs to know, Rose," Rick said, taking her hand. "And he's growing up. You can't stop him from growing up."

Rose shot her husband a sharp look. "I'm not trying to! It's just that…" Rose trailed off, taking a breath and carefully measuring words. "I just believe that when the time is right we will know it. There'll be a sign and we'll know it. Then we'll tell him."

"You're right," Rick squeezed his wife's hand and smiled. "As usual, you're the smart one."

Donut's second favorite activity.

Chapter Three

Discoveries, strange and frightening

"**Y**ou think they'll have food there?" Donut asked as he bounded along beside Ryan down the dark streets of the residential neighborhood. "I mean, they'll probably have hamburgers, but I wonder if they'll have desserts?"

Donut was Ryan's oldest friend, one of the few kids who wasn't bothered by the fact that Ryan didn't talk much. In fact, Donut seemed to like the fact that Ryan's words were spare, because it meant Donut could talk even more.

"Maybe instead of hamburgers they'll have sushi. I could really go for some sushi," Donut continued as he bob-

17

bled a plastic jar in his hands.

Like Ryan, Donut didn't make a lot of friends. His non-stop yammering could be irritating, and he was an expert on many subjects, some of which people found creepy. But his favorite subject was food. Even before Ryan's growth spurt Donut was several inches shorter, but he carried slightly more weight. This gave him a very round torso that some people called stocky.

"I'm pretty sure they won't have sushi," Ryan said.

A full moon shone down as they walked. The jar Donut carried was a former peanut butter canister, now completely cleaned out. Donut had poked a few holes in the lid and put some handfuls of grass inside.

If Ryan were of a mind to think about it, it would be obvious that they were engaging in Donut's second-favorite activity: collecting bugs. But he was barely paying attention to his friend. All he could think about was Corrine's brown eyes and the way it sounded when she said his name earlier, but those queasy feelings of happiness that swirled in his stomach gradually gave way to another feeling.

Ryan knew the feeling well as the hairs on the back of his neck started to stand on end. Without him realizing it, Donut had led him to the far south end of the neighborhood where the old Oobakka ranch house stood.

The house was a large, two-story structure that had been abandoned for as long as Ryan could remember. During the day, it was a dusty, white structure, faded by decades spent in the sun. Somehow, in the dark of night, the house always looked dark gray, almost black.

There were stories in the neighborhood that something terrible had happened there once. A whole family had died under mysterious circumstances. Kids at school claimed that when the police found them, each member of the family had been wrapped up in spider webs and all their blood had sucked out.

Whenever Ryan had to pass by the house, he wanted

to run away as fast as he could. Even though his parents told him the stories weren't true, some part of him believed that they might be.

"W-w-we should turn around," Ryan stammered, hoping Donut couldn't hear how scared he was.

"Don't be a chicken-butt. This is what I wanted to show you."

Donut put his hands on Ryan's back and pushed him forward towards the house. Ryan resisted at first, pushing back with his legs. As his muscles strained against his heavy friend, Ryan remembered what his father often told him. "Most times fear hurts you more than the thing you're afraid of."

"All right," he told Donut, annoyed by his friend's insistence. He walked forward on his own.

The two boys scurried behind a stand of thorn bushes at the edge of the Oobakka property. The bushes were sometimes called crucifixion thorns, and to Ryan they seemed to claw at the full moon like bony hands.

Donut studied the bushes, eyebrows furrowed, a scowl of concentration on his face. He held his plastic jar in one hand and the lid in the other as he studied the bush. Ryan couldn't help thinking that the look of concentration wasn't much different than what he saw on Kirby's face when the cat spotted a nearby bird.

Suddenly Donut sprung his trap, his chubby arms coming together, closing the jar and lid around a leaf on the tree. "Gotcha!"

Donut held the jar up to the moonlight and studied his prize. It was a large spider, the likes of which Ryan had never seen before. It was bigger than most spiders, perhaps four inches long from front leg to back, with a sandy, almost flesh-colored body.

"What kind is it?" Ryan asked.

"I'm convinced it's a new species. Note the tail, not unheard of in the arachnid class, but to have a cluster like this is very unusual," Donut said in a scholarly voice, pointing out the creature's weird tail that split into four or five barbed ends. Donut kept talking, but all Ryan could think about were the stories of the Oobakka family wrapped in webbing. He began to wonder if there were other spiders on that bush.

As fear welled up inside Ryan, he failed to notice that Donut had abruptly stopped talking. Ryan looked at his friend who stared at the Oobakka house, his bottom lip trembling. "R-R-Ryan," Donut stammered quietly.

Ryan followed Donut's gaze to the house. Pinpricks of shock rippled through his body again as he saw a dark figure standing by one of the house's windows, illuminated only by the moonlight. The figure was tall and slender and hunched over, like a skinny old man with bone disease. As the person walked in front of the window the boys saw his bony, slender fingers with long nails that he kept curled in front of him like a praying mantis.

Then the figure reached down with those hands and lifted something off the floor. Ryan wasn't sure what it was at first but soon recognized the small, furry shape as a house cat. The strange old man lifted the cat up above his head and the cat began to moan the horrible sound that it makes when it is terrified, like a baby in distress.

Donut clutched Ryan's arm so hard that both boys fell over as the cat's shrieking reached its peak and suddenly stopped. Through the branches, Ryan could see that the dark figure had disappeared from the window.

"Omigosh, omigosh, omigosh," Donut kept repeating as the boys lay flat on the ground.

It was only from this low vantage point that Ryan realized the boys weren't alone. In the dust just a few feet from his nose was the fat, shiny, black and red tail of a Gila Monster.

The lizard turned its thick head back and hissed, flicking his black, forked tongue at the boys and sending Donut running into the street, screaming. But Ryan was too scared to move.

The town of Gila Flats was named for these intimidating creatures, which lived in the nearby desert. Ryan had seen one or two before, but it was rare to find them in town like this. Although they had a venomous bite, they were very shy and usually stayed away from people. As the lizard turned and continued walking, Ryan could see that it was not the only Gila Monster in the yard. There were perhaps a dozen such reptiles, some twice as big as the first, pacing restlessly in front of the house, looking towards that window, and hissing their eerie hiss.

Ryan felt that same dizzy, disoriented feeling that he had felt when he stumbled across the street to meet Corrine. Suddenly the dry crucifixion thorn bush burst into flames right in front of him, illuminating the eerie march of reptiles.

As he looked around, he saw many more Gila Monsters walking towards the Oobakka house. Beyond them, stocky Donut ran as fast as his thick legs could carry him, and Ryan decided his friend had the right idea as he got up and ran away from the strange procession.

Their unwavering stare

Chapter Four

Things cool off and then boil over

Corrine Babbot's family lived in a large house in the new neighborhood that lay just to the north of Gila Flats. The house's was probably three times the size of any of those found in the old neighborhood, where kids like Ryan lived. The yard had thick green grass, a rarity in Gila Flats. Corrine's pool party was underway and now that all her girlfriends were here, she wanted to show off the new toy.

"I'm so sure," Dawn said, rolling her eyes in mock disgust. "Your birthday isn't for another month."

"I know," replied Corrine, "But Dad wanted me to have it now."

The "it" Corrine was referring to was the brand new motor scooter that she currently sat atop. The scooter was modern and sleek, with a long seat perfect for two riders, and every inch of it was a hot pink color that made Corrine squint when she looked at it in the sunlight. She continued, "Because if I have the scooter now then your parents might get a brainstorm to get one for you too!"

Dawn let out a devilish giggle. "We'll be the scooter chicks of Gila Flats."

"No more waiting for our parents to pick us up after school. We'll ride in and out of town together."

"And you can just roll up and visit your boyfriend, Ryan," Dawn teased.

"Shut it," Corrine responded, hoping her sharp tone would cover the fact that it actually had occurred to her that she might see more of Ryan with her newfound mobility. But just where was he?

Corrine looked around the yard. Twenty or so kids from school played in the large, in-ground pool. Others lined up for hamburgers near a gas grill run by Mr. Babbot. And then, Ryan entered the yard with a short, stocky boy she recognized from school, and two people who must have been his parents.

She smiled, as Ryan looked her way. The boy awkwardly and hurriedly shooed his mother and father out of the yard before turning back and meeting her gaze. He smiled and waved.

"Speak of the devil and he appears," deadpanned Dawn.

* * *

Ryan tried to keep his composure as Corrine approached, looking cute in her one-piece swimsuit "I'm really glad you came, Ryan," she beamed.

"We wouldn't have missed it," Donut responded for his friend, extending a hand to Corrine, who graciously shook it. "My name's Donald, but everybody calls me Donut."

"Nice to know you, Donut," Corrine giggled.

"That's an unusual name."

"Yeah, I'm Ryan's best friend," Donut said. Ryan groaned silently. There was no turning off the chatter machine now. "I like bugs. I have a big collection. Last week I found a Polyphemus Moth. It has, like, eyes on its wings."

"Hence the name, Polyphemus," Corrine chimed in. "After the Cyclops of Greek Mythology, known for his prominent eye."

"Yeah. Me and Ryan, we hang out all the time," Donut blathered on, barely acknowledging Corrine's remark. "We discovered a new species of arachnid the other night. Did he tell you that? It was at the Oobakka ranch. I thought the old place was abandoned but it seems like there's someone in there."

"Well, the Peters are here," Corrine offered, pointing to the Peters family who sat on folding chairs under the shade of one of the larger trees. Mr. and Mrs. Peters and their son, Jason sat nearly motionless, their heads tilted lazily to the side as if they'd just woken from a nap.

"Mrs. Peters sells houses. Maybe we should ask if she

sold it to someone…" Corrine said, trailing off. They were far enough away that the Peters shouldn't have been able to hear them. Yet, when their name was mentioned, all three roused from their sleepy trance in unison, turned their heads, and stared right at Ryan. He felt more than a little unnerved by their unwavering stare.

"Yeah, anyhow, I'm calling the spider a scourge-tail, on account of it having this weird tail cluster with stingers on it," Donut blurted out, breaking Ryan from his stare down with the Peters. "At least I think they're stingers. The tail flicks around like this and-"

Corrine's faced squinched up in disgust as Donut wiggled his finger in and out, emulating the tail as he described his discovery. Dead certain that Corrine was about to walk away and never speak to him again, Ryan knew he had to do something.

"Donut," Ryan exclaimed, silencing his friend. "Did you see they're putting pineapple slices on the hamburgers?"

And Donut abruptly spun around and headed for the grill. "I'm all over the pineburger."

Ryan smiled at Corrine and shrugged. "Sorry about that. He kinda loves bugs, you know? Sounds like you know something about them too."

"Bugs can be interesting sometimes," Corrine said, laughing. "I mean, it's cool that somebody knows about something besides what was on TV last night. But mythology is really my subject. Cyclops, Ulysses. It's like comic books with togas."

Ryan laughed, and once again felt that strange, spotty feeling as he looked at Corrine's beautiful smile. He forced himself to look away and quickly remembered his manners. "Thanks for inviting me here. I was kind of surprised when you did."

"I've seen you around school a lot," Corrine said. "That's dumb. I mean, of course I did. There aren't that many kids at our school. But I've seen you, you know? So many times I thought, this time he's going to say hi to me."

Embarrassment started to creep into Ryan's heart.

"But then," she continued, playfully slipping her arm around Ryan's, "I thought, maybe he just needs a little help.

Maybe it wouldn't cause the earth to split open and swallow us if I went ahead and said hi first."

And Ryan's admiration for Corrine grew ten times more. He'd never felt so comfortable with someone in such a short period of time.

"Now come on," Corrine said, now leading him by the hand to the pool. It was a large, in-ground model filled with cool, blue water. Everywhere kids from school splashed around. "You wore your trunks, right? Let's swim!"

Corrine led Ryan right to the pool and dove in ahead of him. Ryan laughed as he peeled off his baggy shorts, revealing his swim trunks underneath. He jumped into the pool after her.

The moment he hit the surface, the water felt like icy daggers against Ryan's skin. He couldn't believe all these kids were playing in this freezing water. He quickly came up for air, his skin covered in gooseflesh, and hugged his arms against his body.

Corrine swam back to him and splashed him playfully. "Isn't the water great?"

"Y-y-yeah," Ryan said, trying to keep his teeth from chattering. He didn't want Corrine to see how awkward and out of place he felt.

"You're not cold, are you?" Corrine teased, and as she ran her hand up and down Ryan's arm, that strange feeling returned. Dots danced before his eyes, and it felt as if somebody had turned the pool over on its side.

Corrine suddenly jumped back, pulling her hand away and staring at it with a frown. From Ryan's woozy perspective, it seemed as if she'd been drawn miles away from him.

"Your arm is so warm," she said, but Ryan could barely hear her. A low rumble filled his ears, and he

34

suddenly realized that the water around him was starting to bubble and churn.

He could see Corrine talking to him, but couldn't hear her words over the strange rumbling in his ears, or the churning of the water. The rest of Corrine's friends turned their attention to Ryan, and he noticed that the entire pool was now bubbling like a hot tub.

The world tilted again and this time the kids dropped away from Ryan until all he saw was the blue Arizona sky, and then suddenly he was underwater. Through the rippling surface Ryan could see everyone scrambling out of the pool. Some of the girls' muffled screams filtered through to Ryan's ears.

Ryan no longer felt cold. He was perfectly comfortable and relaxed floating in the churning hot tub that had been a swimming pool, and the dark dots filled his vision until his entire world became black and silent.

It looked like the road had just collapsed into an underground cave.

Chapter Five

The word and the crater

The gentle rocking of the Rick Morales' jeep and the steady hum of tires on the blacktop coaxed Ryan back into the world. As he slowly opened his eyes, he mumbled a word. Ryan had never heard the word before. He didn't know what it meant, but it seemed to stick in his head and perch on his tongue, waiting to be set free.

"Akashalon," Ryan's voice was weak and the word came out as barely a whisper, but it was loud enough get the attention of his mother, who rode in the front seat.

"Ryan? You're awake," Mom said, turning in her seat to watch him intently. She looked very worried, and Ryan knew she wasn't playing any games this time. "Rick!

He's awake!"

Dad turned his head away from the road and flashed his son a warm smile. "What did you say, Ryan?" his father asked before returning his focus to his driving.

Ryan sat up in his seat and Mom reached over and hugged him. "Are you O.K., Ryan?"

Outside the car window, Ryan saw they were on Highway 87, which connected the center of Gila Flats with the new housing development where Corrine lived. All around them were miles of desert with the purple-orange sky of the setting sun above. "Mom? Dad? What happened?"

"Don't you remember, son?" Dad asked.

"Something happened to the Babbot's pool. They think it was the water heater," Mom said. She tried not to show how worried she was, but tears welled in her eyes. "Are you sure you're O.K.?"

"I feel fine, Mom. It's O.K.," Ryan said. He looked over his torso and arms and saw nothing wrong. But one thing wasn't O.K. with Ryan. He couldn't help worrying that what had happened was his fault. "Was anyone hurt?"

"All the kids got out of the pool when it started heating up. Nobody was hurt except–" his mother's voice cracked a little bit. "They said you fainted. You were floating in the water, and it was over one hundred degrees."

"What did I do?" Ryan asked quietly, but his question was cut short as his father brought the Jeep to an abrupt stop.

"What the heck?" Dad craned his neck to try and see what was causing the traffic jam up ahead.

There were never traffic jams on Highway 87. Ryan knew they were usually lucky to see two other cars on the road from downtown Gila Flats to the new suburbs in the north. There just wasn't much reason to be on the highway.

Rick turned off the Jeep. "Wait here," he told Rose and Ryan, who promptly ignored him as all three of them got out of the car. Rick stood on the Jeep's bumper, Rose craned her neck and Ryan climbed up on the hood, giving him the best vantage point to see what was causing the hold-up.

"Wow," Ryan muttered. Highway 87 now ended abruptly at an enormous crater in the desert floor, which was perhaps twice as wide as the two-lane road. Ryan didn't know what could cause such a thing. It looked like the road had just collapsed into an underground cave.

On either side of the crater, cars beeped in frustration. Other drivers tried to maneuver around the mysterious hole that hadn't been there just a half-hour earlier when Ryan's parents had passed through there.

"Come on," Mom said as she helped Ryan down. They got back in the car while Dad talked with another motorist.

Ryan sat in the back seat and tried to make sense of everything that had happened: the boiling pool, the crater, his dizzy spells, and even the burning thorn bush and crowd of Gila Monsters from the other night.

As Ryan pondered all of the recent strangeness, he noticed a slender, hairy shape, like a pipe cleaner, gently tap the outside of the car window where he sat. A second one appeared next to it. Soon Ryan could see that these were the legs of Donut's new scourge-tail spider. Not the same one his friend had captured, but the same kind of spider.

Ryan shuddered, but was weirdly mesmerized as the creature silently moved up the window towards the opening at the top.

He saw the creature's weird split tail, with its multiple hooked endings almost scraping along the glass.

The thing would be inside the car in a few seconds if he didn't do something! Ryan hurriedly cranked the window handle. The spider rode the closing window up until it sealed shut. It silently probed the seal on the window, looking for a way into the car.

Ryan started at the sound of the door slamming as his Father entered the Jeep and started the engine. "Let's go," Dad said and pulled the car out of traffic and out onto the dry, dusty desert.

Ryan watched the weird bug cling to the glass as the wind from the moving Jeep whipped at the spider until it couldn't hold on any longer. In a blink, the scourge-tail was gone.

Ryan's father drove past the traffic jam and then around the outskirts of the crater. As they passed, Ryan tried to look down into the pit. At the bottom was a large hole that seemed filled with blackness, as if it led down to the very core of the Earth itself.

Just as they had the night before, dozens of Gila Monsters had gathered around the crater, their forked tongues flicking as they slowly marched down towards the ominous hole.

"Ryan." His mother's voice seemed to creep in from

afar. "I want you to tell your father what you said."

"What I said?" Ryan repeated. He didn't understand what Mom meant.

"When you woke up. You said a word. Do you remember?"

As Ryan watched the army of Gilas and the giant hole recede into the distance, a strange sense of comfort overcame him and he recalled the word that had sprung into his mind, uninvited.

"Akashalon."

"That's troubling."

Chapter Six

Things change for Donut and Ryan

onut paced around the front room of his empty house. His parents weren't home yet. They had expected him to be at the party for several more hours, but he had arrived home early after Ryan collapsed in the pool.

A sick feeling filled up Donut's stomach. He looked in the refrigerator, hoping to find a snack to push that sensation away, but he quickly realized he had no appetite. It wasn't hunger he felt, but worry over what had happened to his best friend.

Ryan's fainting spell had brought the pool party to an abrupt close as parents had hurriedly sent all the kids home while they summoned help for Ryan. Donut had been forced

to accept a ride back home with some other kids' folks. He felt that it was extremely unfair of them to send him away, seeing as he was Ryan's best friend and all. With that thought Donut's worry mixed with frustration and created a new queasy sensation.

Looking for something to distract him, he leafed through a small book titled *Insects of Southern Argentina.* Donut had a reputation for getting lost in books like this one, reading for hours until he had absorbed entire volumes cover to cover. Yet, at this moment the book held no interest. Donut could only worry about his friend.

He spied the glass terrarium sitting on small table nearby. There were several of these throughout the house, each terrarium a miniature forest or stream housing a prized insect find. This one was the new home of his strange scourge-tail spider. Surely some observation of the "arachnid find of the century," as he was certain it would be referred to in the science journals, would take his mind off things.

Donut squinted and peered through the glass,

hoping for a glimpse of the spider. The few small plants in it were now tented with thick, dark spider webs. He could not see the creature, which must have been hiding underneath. He tapped on the glass but still could not see the specimen or any signs of movement within.

"That's troubling," said Donut out loud, even though there was nobody around to hear. Deciding that he'd better take a closer look, Donut lifted the terrarium's lid, being careful not to disturb the intricately spun webs beneath. He frowned, noting that there was now a tear in the lid's thin nylon mesh.

As he examined the damage a small shape popped up from the webbing and skittered across, startling Donut and jangling his nerves. The little scourge-tail spider rested atop the webs and stared up at him, it's tail flipping around menacingly.

Donut heaved a huge sigh and laughed at himself. Maybe it was the spider and maybe it was his concern over Ryan, but he was certainly on edge tonight. The little creature had actually frightened him.

The spider looked to be in good health so Donut placed the lid back on the terrarium, watching his tiny specimen to make sure it didn't try to scurry out at the wrong time. More than one specimen had lost a leg that way.

As the lid clicked back into place Donut saw something out of the corner of his eye. He turned his head just in time to see another scourge-tail racing down the wall on eight furry legs. The spider stopped at the same level as Donut's eyes, which were wide with amazement. There were two of them!

And it was then that Donut discovered the scourge-tail spider's amazing ability to leap across great distances. The spider shot from the wall like a dart and landed on Donut's face, before skittering up through his hair and down the back of his head.

Donut screamed loudly in the dim house but again, there was no one around to hear him.

* * *

As the Morales family piled out of their car, Ryan noticed Mrs. Wilkensen sitting in the dusk on the front porch of her house.

"Ryan," Mrs. Wilkensen called. She was amazingly cheerful, although her eyes looked tired and droopy. In fact, the old woman looked as if she was moments away from falling asleep. She pulled her shawl up around her neck and asked, "Why don't you bring that nice cat over? I do love a good cat."

She waved a listless hand at them. Ryan's parents smiled at her. They seemed pleasantly surprised by her friendly gesture, but he found the idea of Mrs. Wilkensen being nice or inviting Kirby over strangely unnerving.

"Come into the house, Ryan," Dad said, putting

an arm around his son's shoulders. "We've got something to tell you."

* * *

"Where did you hear that word, Ryan?" Mom asked intently.

Ryan sat on an armchair in their air-conditioned house, his hand stroking Kirby's soft fur and feeling the rumble of the cat's contented purr. His parents sat on the couch across from him. Ryan couldn't recall the last time he'd seen them so serious. In between all of them was a coffee table with a wooden jewelry box on it that Ryan had never seen before.

"I don't know," Ryan answered. "I don't think I've ever heard it before. It was just in my head when I woke up."

"Ryan, there's something we have to tell you," his father said, speaking slowly and precisely. "We always aimed to tell you at some point, but we were never sure when the right time would be."

"We think that time is now, Ryan," Mom said, a warm smile on her face. "I'll just come right out with it: We're not your true parents."

The words seemed to bounce away from Ryan, like baseball taking a bad hop, and he couldn't quite get a handle on them. "What?" he asked, his face screwed up with confusion.

"Your birth parents, she means," answered Dad. "We're your Mom and Dad, of course."

"Nothing can change that," his mother chimed in. "But you didn't come to us the way most kids come to their folks."

Ryan's head spun. With all the weirdness that had been going around, he wasn't sure how to take this news. He felt like he should be upset, but he wasn't. He wasn't even sure he knew what they were saying. "I don't understand."

"Rick, maybe you should start at the beginning," Mom said.

Ryan's father nodded and stood. He looked at his son and then paced the floor for a moment. Then he turned back to Ryan and looked the boy in the eye.

"Ryan, before I start, I just want you to know that your Mom and I...we love you. You're our son and our pride and joy. Nothing I'm about to say changes that. You hear?"

Ryan tried to quiet the small sense of dread that swirled in the pit of his stomach. Of course he knew his folks were his folks. He didn't need to be told. He loved them too. He just wished his father would get on with his story.

"One day," Dad began, "Some thirteen or so years ago is where I reckon I ought to start. That was the day I first met you, Ryan.

"I was doing my job, same as every day, driving my Jeep along the border and making sure everything was on the up and up. Truth is, the job can be pretty dull at times, and many days all I see are blue skies, white sun, and the open desert. None of that requires my attention on a regular basis.

"Anyhow, as I drove along, I saw a small mound off in the distance. Now, people sometimes pile up rocks out

"Some darn fool had left a child out there in the desert."

there in the desert to help mark their way when they travel. That's on account of there not being many landmarks out there. They're called cairns.

"So, I went over to check it out. It's part of the job. Sometimes the wrong people build these cairns for the wrong reasons. My job would be to log it and maybe take the mound away. So I drove on over to it.

"I can't really describe the feeling as I got close and realized it wasn't a mound at all. I wasn't sure if I was angry or sad or afraid or some combination of all of those. What I found wasn't a cairn at all…

"It seemed to me some darn fool had left a child out there in the desert. It was you, Ryan, and you were just a baby, lying there in the blistering hot son with no clothes and nothing but dust all around.

"Now, I've seen some terrible things in my job. I've seen people get stranded in the desert, and that sun is not forgiving. It can take a healthy, grown man down fast and I could only imagine what it had done to this poor child, and God only knew how long this child had been out there.

"I went to you Ryan and, if I'm being honest, I didn't really expect the best. I just couldn't imagine a baby surviving for more than an hour. But when I bent down to pick you up your eyes popped open and I'll be darned if you didn't beam the most beautiful smile at me that I'd ever seen.

"I was so happy you were O.K., so relieved, I believe I bawled like a little girl all the way back to the Jeep as I thanked God and whoever else it was that brought you to us."

Ryan watched his mother smile at his father as both of his parents wiped tears from their eyes. "We just knew you were meant for us, Ryan," Mom said. "You were a miracle, and we were meant to find you."

Ryan felt some measure of relief. He thought his parents were about to tell him something terrible, but as they had promised, this story really didn't change anything. "But, why tell me now?"

Ryan's father regained his composure and continued. "Ryan, we always knew you were a bit different. First off, surviving in the desert like you did."

"Once, when you were three, you touched a hot iron. It should have burned your hand, but it didn't," Mom added.

"There were a handful of things...times when any person would have been hurt or burned...but not you," Dad said. "You seem to have a special relationship with heat."

"Like heating up a swimming pool," Mom said.

"Or melting ice cream...or burning a thorn bush," Ryan continued.

Ryan's father picked up the jewelry box. "There were a few other things about that day in the desert," he said, opening the box and taking out a thin leather cord with a stone hanging from the end of it. "You were wearing this around your neck."

As Ryan took the stone from

his dad, he felt a tingle of heat pass through his hand and run up his arm. The stone was a kind of amulet, thick and flat, with a rough texture on one side. One edge of it was round, like a coin, but it had two straight edges as well, like a slice from a pie that had been cut into four equal pieces. In the corner of the wedge was a red crystal.

On the smooth side of the stone was a carved symbol, round on the bottom and left side, but curved up to a point with jagged lines on the right. To Ryan it looked like a fireball.

"There was one other thing out there in the desert that day," Ryan's father said. "Whoever put you there, they drew some kind of circle in the sand. It looked almost like a ritual circle…like it was meant to protect you. There were letters all around the edge of it.

"Put together, the letters spelled Akashalon."

The sphere glowed yellow and pulsed like a tiny sun.

Chapter Seven

Akashalon

Ryan lay on his bed and examined the amulet, dangling it by the leather cord so it hung just inches in front of his face. A warm breeze blew in as moonlight poured into his open bedroom window and refracted through the red crystal on the amulet.

Next to Ryan's pillow, Kirby had curled up in a fuzz ball and snored into his ear. Ryan envied his cat. He wanted to sleep, but there were so many questions running through his head that it was impossible.

Still something about the red crystal was soothing, almost hypnotic. Ryan stared at it as it turned in the moonlight. Ryan imagined the crystal growing huge…so big

he could pass through its walls like a ghost and enter it.

Suddenly his daydream was interrupted as a tiny glowing sphere appeared in the space between Ryan's eyes and the crystal. The sphere glowed yellow and pulsed like a tiny sun. Ryan watched in amazement as a red flare grew from its top and the sphere became an orange pillar of fire, dancing in front of the crystal. As it burned, Ryan could just make out a quiet whispering noise that seemed to come from the flames.

Am I doing that? he wondered, awestruck.

Another flare snaked out from the pillar and passed into the crystal, just as Ryan had imagined doing himself. It seemed the miniature flame was feeding energy into the crystal and, slowly but steadily, a flickering glow formed on the other side.

Tiny tendrils of orange and gold flame were snaking through the crystal and forming shapes in the air above Ryan's bed. Lines of fire floated and joined each other, like a drawing taking shape.

As this happened, the quiet hiss of the fire grew in

intensity. Ryan listened as the hiss seemed to take a more distinct form of its own. It now sounded like hundreds of tiny voices, all trying to speak in unison, but he couldn't understand what they were saying.

And an image formed in the flames that floated in the air, and Ryan saw a city, a beautiful golden city unlike anything he'd seen on TV or in books. He'd certainly never seen anything like it in real life.

The buildings weren't square like normal buildings, but rather had strange curved shapes and overhangs that seemed to defy gravity. There were small structures at the edge of the city, which gradually got taller and taller as they built towards a huge tower at the center.

The city was alive. In the vision, there were people moving about, working, smiling, interacting...playing. They all seemed happy and content. And while Ryan had never seen anything like it before, he knew the name of the city even before the tiny voices of the flame whispered it...

Akashalon!

The place was beautiful and fascinating. Glowing

Akashalon!

with life, it somehow looked like it belonged in both a medieval fantasy and a science fiction movie. Then, just as suddenly as the city had appeared in this illusion, it started to go dark.

Ryan frowned as one by one, the buildings on the edges of the city turned black. Like a disease, the darkness spread towards the center. Ryan's apprehension increased as gloomy netting formed over the dark areas and extended towards the buildings that still shimmered with light and people.

"No," Ryan whispered as he recognized that this murky blanket was a giant spider's web. When he looked more closely, he saw that the webs covering the dark areas of the city squirmed and crawled with sinister forms...like large, human-sized spiders.

The darkness spread over Akashalon as its buildings were overwhelmed by the spider webs, until the only place left standing was the tower in the center. And although Ryan had only known the city for a few moments, he felt sickened and sad as he watched the dark webs work their way up the tower and extinguish Akashalon's bright hopeful flame.

"No," Ryan cried out, overwhelmed by his anger. "Make them stop! Save them!"

Suddenly the flickering illusion of the city turned into a blinding white light that filled the room. Ryan squeezed his eyes shut and felt intense heat all around him. When he opened his eyes, he was horrified to realize that his room was on fire!

"No! Not my house," Ryan yelled.

"...*as you command*...," said the quiet, whispering voice of the flame.

"Don't burn my house!"

Ryan screamed and sat bolt upright in his bed. He looked around at his room, but everything was dark and quiet. Nothing seemed out of place. Was it all just a dream? he wondered.

Ryan opened his hand and realized he had been clutching the amulet so hard that the little flame symbol had become imprinted on his palm.

Sweating and thirsty, he stumbled through the dark

hallway and into the bathroom for a glass of water. Closing the door, he turned on the light and only then realized that he was wearing the charred rags of what had been his pajamas. The edges were brown and smoldering, as if they had been burned off him.

He found Kirby on the floor, hunkered down behind the cool porcelain of the toilet. The frightened cat's whiskers were curled up and singed, but that cat was unharmed, although he mewed pitifully at Ryan.

"It really did happen…"

"Don't be afraid, Ryan."

Chapter Eight

Brain Stingers

When Donut answered the door he looked as if he had just woken up. His eyes were heavy-lidded and bleary. Ryan thought his friend had probably spent the night with a book. That wasn't anything unusual.

What was unusual, however, was the sight of Donut wearing a turtleneck shirt. With the recent hot weather, Ryan thought the shirt looked awfully uncomfortable, and the beads of sweat on Donut's face confirmed this.

"Up all night reading again, huh?" Ryan asked, smiling at his friend.

"Nah. No sleep," was Donut's groggy reply. "Strange, strange dreams. Spiders… webs…"

Donut trailed off, his eyes staring away from Ryan, who had never known his friend to be at a loss for words. "Well, I've got something I want to show you," Ryan said.

Donut invited Ryan inside, shuffling ahead of him before collapsing on a chair. Ryan shuddered at the creepy sight of Donut's web-filled terrarium on the nearby table, recalling his vision from the previous evening. He decided it was best to get down to business.

"My parents told me this weird story last night. It turns out that I'm, like, adopted or something," Ryan began, although Donut looked like he was about to nod off at any minute. His head lolled to the side and his glazed eyes seemed to focus on nothing in particular.

For whatever reason, Donut seemed devoid of his natural curiosity, and Ryan though he'd better get right to the good stuff. Ryan reached inside the neck of his t-shirt and pulled out the amulet. He'd been wearing it ever since the strange incident the night before.

"My dad gave me this and I…"

Donut's sleepy eyes popped wide open at the sight of

the amulet, and the boy suddenly sprang to life. "You!" he shouted, jumping to his feet and pointing. "You!"

Ryan cringed back on the couch, alarmed by his friend's sudden animated display.

Donut saw the look on Ryan's face and quickly regained his composure. "You…you…you gotta see something," Donut started. His hands quivered nervously as he tried not to point at his friend again. "Remember that spider we found? You gotta see this!"

Donut turned away from Ryan and went to the spider-webbed terrarium, where he lifted the lid from it. It was then that Ryan saw a strange lump, almost the size of an egg, bulging under the turtleneck collar on the back of Donut's neck. As Ryan stared at the lump, an icy feeling formed in the pit of his stomach as he realized the lump was moving… squirming… like something alive!

Ryan's surprised expression turned to one of complete horror when Donut turned around, holding not one, but two of the scourge-tail spiders in his hands. "Don't be afraid, Ryan," Donut said, advancing on his friend.

"D-D-Donut?" Ryan questioned. Clearly his friend wasn't himself.

"They're really cool," Donut said, just as the two spiders leaped at Ryan's face! Before he could even scream, a tiny puff of flame appeared in front of him and knocked both scourge-tails to the ground, their legs waving in the air.

Ryan didn't wait around for them to stand back up. Panicked, he bolted out the front door of the house and ran as fast as his legs would carry him.

* * *

In record time, Ryan dashed through the old neighborhood and arrived at his house. He threw open the front door and entered into the cool confines of his air-conditioned home.

He almost slammed right into his mother, who stood there in the living room, a giant smile on her face. Maybe it was because of what happened with Donut, but that big smile just made him more nervous.

"Ryan," Mom said serenely, staring at him with tired eyes. "We're so glad you're back."

Ryan noticed that his mother wore a light scarf that he'd never seen before around her neck. He thought of Donut and his turtleneck. The sound of the front door slamming startled Ryan, and he realized his father, who should have been at work, was standing behind him.

"M-Mom? Dad?" Ryan asked, and they both smiled that same weird grin at him.

"Just locking up," Dad said slowly and deliberately as he fumbled with the tricky deadbolt.

"Ryan, you're just in time for dinner," Mom said cheerfully.

Ryan glanced at the clock on the wall and saw that it was only quarter after three. "Isn't it a little early?" he asked.

"Nonsense. I'm starved," his father said, and continued struggling with the bolt. "Have you seen the cat?"

"Come on, son," Mom said and Ryan followed her into the kitchen. His parents were definitely acting weird, just like Donut. Ryan eyed the house's side door, which opened into a foyer near the kitchen.

"We've got something special for you," Mom said, her eyes drifting to one side with that sleepy, unfocused look. She shuffled past the kitchen table and opened a cupboard. Standing on her tiptoes, she reached for something on the top shelf.

As she strained to reach inside, her scarf slipped off, and what Ryan saw underneath filled him with a feeling of horror more intense than anything he'd felt before. Clinging to the back of his mother's neck was another scourge-tail! Each prong of its tail was stuck into her skin, as if it had stung all the way into her spine.

Finally Ryan's mother reached what she was after. When she turned back to the kitchen table, she was holding a deep, rectangular plastic container. Inside, dark, eight-legged shapes skittered around.

"Ryan?" The wide, fake smile dipped from her face as Rick entered the room. They looked at the open side door of the house and saw that Ryan was gone.

* * *

Ryan dashed up the main street of Gila Flats, his heart pounding in his chest. Mom, Dad, Donut...even Mrs. Wilkensen...everyone was acting so weird. They must all have one of those spiders on the backs of their necks. It was like they were stinging people's brains. They were brain-stingers. What was he going to do?

Ryan remembered the illusion of Akashalon that had appeared in his room and how it had seemed to be overrun and destroyed by spiders. He thought about that weird scourge-tail that clung to the window of his father's car. His imagination ran wild and he could almost see one of them crawling up his back and driving that stinger into his spine. Would he fall into that same, sleepy daze like everyone else?

Ryan dashed to the one safe place he had left. *Please don't let them have Albert*, he thought as threw open the glass door of the ice cream shop. He came to a screeching stop as his sneakers hit the tile floor.

There sat Albert, the would-be cowboy, slumped over on a bar stool in front of the soda counter. His head hung down as if he were asleep.

Ryan wasn't sure what to do. *Maybe Albert is just asleep*, he thought.

"There's been a lot of whispering on the web," the old man said in a low, croaking voice that sent made Ryan's stomach lurch with fear. Albert slowly raised his head up and met Ryan's stare with his own, drowsy eyes. "We've been searching for you, little Fire Prince."

One by one, the brain-stingers appeared on the glass front of the soda counter and skittered up to the top. Ryan stared in wide-eyed terror as he realized there were dozens, maybe hundreds of spiders massing on the counter behind Albert.

Ryan bolted out the door. He stole a glance back and saw Albert shamble out of his shop, a swarm of spiders spilling around his legs like a rushing wave of gray water.

Ryan ran down the main street of Gila Flats, but where could he go? The spiders had his parents. They had his friends. There was nowhere left, and now Albert and his arachnid legion were doggedly pursuing him. Ryan just ran blindly.

Rounding a corner, he ran into the roaring engine and pink metal and plastic that was Corrine's motor scooter, which sent him stumbling backward until he sat down in the middle of the street.

"Ryan, are you O.K.?" Corrine asked, her eyes red-rimmed with tears. "I need help. Everyone is acting weird."

Ryan looked back and saw Albert walking towards them, a river of brain-stingers undulating around him. Corrine followed his gaze and began screaming. "Ryan! Get on!"

Ryan stood up, but after what had happened with Donut, Mom and Dad, he wasn't taking any chances. He felt he already knew the truth, but he reached out for the long, soft, blond hair that ran down Corrine's

back and lifted it up.

"What are you doing? Get on the scooter!" Corrine shouted, her voice edged with panic.

Ryan saw that there was no spider clinging to Corrine's neck. He breathed a sigh of relief and sat down behind her on the scooter's long seat. Corrine gunned the engine took off with a squeal of rubber, leaving Albert and his spiders far behind.

"I'm no hero."

Chapter Nine

The Fire Prince

Ryan looked up at the bright field of stars over the desert sky. He and Corrine had zoomed out of town as fast as they could. When they reached the giant hole in the middle of the highway, they decided to stop. Corrine sat in rapt attention, twirling Ryan's fire amulet in her fingers, as he told her the whole story.

He told her about the spiders he and Donut found. About the weird guy at the Oobakka ranch house. About what happened after the party. He told her about his father finding him, as an infant, in the desert, thriving in the sun. He told her about the illusion of fire and about the strange encounters with Donut and Mrs. Wilkensen and his parents and everything else leading up to their collision on Main Street.

Ryan felt a little awkward telling his story at first. It all seemed so outlandish to him that even he thought they sounded like lies. He wasn't sure if Corrine would believe any of it, but as he looked into her eyes, he saw she believed every word.

"Wow! It's like the invasion of the cat-eating, body-snatching brain-stingers or something," she whispered in awe. "And you...you're like some...some...Greek hero or something."

"I'm no hero," Ryan said, thinking about how he had left his parents and friends to the spiders.

"No...think about it," Corrine said, grabbing his arm. "What did Albert call you? The Fire Prince. Maybe you're like, a lost heir of the Fire King and Queen."

Ryan smiled at her, "I know you just listened to my

dumb story, but do you know how crazy that sounds?"

"Is it any crazier than a zillion spiders coming to Albert's shop for a scoop of Rocky Road?" Corrine demanded. "And what about the voices in your bedroom. They said, 'as you command.' That's like a royal decree."

"A decree? To who?"

Corrine sighed in exasperation. She stood up and took Ryan's hand and led him to a nearby tumbleweed. "Ryan, I want you to trust me. I read a lot. I think that maybe you are some kind of Fire Prince, like Albert said. I think you made the fire in your room and you made the water in my pool boil. I think you can make things burn."

"Come on, Corrine," Ryan said, shyly. "I can't do all that stuff."

She pulled his hand and guided him over to the tumbleweed. "Just concentrate on this dried up old thing. Picture it burning and it'll happen."

Ryan focused on the bush. In his mind, he pictured

the tumbleweed burning. He imagined the flames licking up to the sky and lighting the whole desert around them. He could almost feel the heat from the image in his mind, "Burn, bush," he commanded, but nothing happened.

He closed his eyes tightly and conjured up the mental picture again. He clenched his fists and balled his

stomach into a knot. "Burn, tumbleweed!" he shouted and grimaced until his face turned purple.

"BURN!" he yelled, hearing his voice echo in the distance as the tumbleweed sat in the dirt in the most unfirey way possible.

"Yeah, that didn't work," Corrine deadpanned. She paced around, her brow furrowed. "I was so sure. I just know that somehow you can do this."

Ryan stared at the stubborn tumbleweed as she paced and murmured. He had believed it too, yet he couldn't seem to make it happen. What was the voice he heard in his bedroom? Had it really said, 'as you command'?

Suddenly Ryan understood. "I don't command the bush," he whispered.

"Burn the bush," he shouted, and a bright orange flame exploded from him and engulfed the tumbleweed.

Corrine grinned and laughed with excitement. "I knew it! Yes!"

Ryan grinned back at her for a second before realizing his sleeve was also on fire! "Not my clothes. Don't burn my clothes!"

And just as suddenly, the flame on his jacket was gone.

"That's it!" Corrine repeated excitedly. "You command the fire! See, you're a hero!"

"Heroes don't run out of town on their girlfriend's scooter," Ryan said with a frown as he sat on a boulder at the edge of the crater.

"Oh," Corrine smiled. "Girlfriend, is it?"

Corrine sat down close to him and leaned over as if to kiss him. Ryan immediately got nervous again. He looked into Corrine's eyes as she moved closer and hoped he wouldn't do anything stupid. But instead, she abruptly started screaming.

Before Ryan knew what was going on, a brain-stinger leaped up from the rock they were sitting on

and landed on Corrine's shirt. She fell onto the ground, but the weird spider clung to her, trying to crawl toward her neck. Corrine twisted and swatted at the bug, but its multi-barbed stinger was whipping wildly at her hands. "Ryan! Help!"

Instinctively Ryan gestured at the spider and said, "Burn the spider," but nothing happened.

"Ryan!" Corrine yelled as the spider tried to walk to her back.

But before Ryan had time to do anything, a Gila about two feet long rushed out of the darkness and pounced on the girl! The spider skittered around just in time for the Gila to snatch it up in its wide jaws and jump back down into the dirt. Still screaming, Corinne crab walked backwards into Ryan's legs.

The Gila paused and looked at the pair, who stared back at it in stunned shock. The spider legs still twisted in its mouth as the reptile threw its head back and swallowed the creepy bug. Then it turned and disappeared into the night.

"Eww. That. Was. GROSS!" Corrine said, shouting the last word. Ryan helped her to her feet.

"But, it did kinda save you," Ryan said with some small admiration for the lizard.

"So, those Gila Monsters eat the spiders?"

"That must be why they were here yesterday," Ryan

said. He felt like pieces of the puzzle were suddenly starting to fit together.

"They came to eat the bugs," Corrine said, staring down into the pit. "Ryan, let's get out of here."

"Yeah, and I think I know where to go."

The whole town was slowly shuffling towards them.

Chapter Ten

"Behold...the Mygantuan!"

"**S**ee? They're still here," Ryan said as they watched the dozen or so Gila Monsters mill around under the full moon in front of the Oobakka house.

He and Corrine had ditched the pink scooter at the edge of town so they could sneak through the southern neighborhood of Gila Flats on foot. "And this is where you found the brain-stinger?" Corrine asked.

Ryan shuddered as he realized that the one Donut had captured that day was probably the same one clinging to the back of his neck right now, controlling him. "Yeah," Ryan replied, "and that old, freaky guy who ate the cat. I think he has something do with all this."

"The guy who moved into the haunted house where the last family was found wrapped in spider webs, just days before the whole town is overrun by mind-controlling spiders?" Corrine echoed mockingly. "You think?"

Ryan smiled at her. As crazy as everything was, Corrine could still make him laugh.

But then Albert's voice croaked from behind them. "Fun time's over, kids. It's time for both of you to join us."

Ryan and Corrine whirled around to see a large mob of people appearing in the street. Albert was at the forefront, with Donut, Rick, and Rose standing to either side of him and dozens more townsfolk behind them. It seemed like the whole town was slowly shuffling towards the two kids.

Ryan looked around nervously. They were surrounded on all sides, with the only refuge being the Oobakka house behind them.

"Don't come any closer, you spider-bitten freaks. He's the Fire Prince," Corrine yelled, pointing at Ryan.

"Yes," Donut hissed quietly. "The Fire Prince."

"Get the Fire Prince," Ryan's mother said, and the mob slowly closed in on them.

"That was good," Ryan said. Grabbing Corrine by the hand, he pulled her through the front gate of the creepy yard.

The Gilas that had congregated there all turned their heads in unison to watch Ryan pass on his way to the porch. Then they moved into a protective line around the porch. The old fence that surrounded the yard buckled and cracked as the whole neighborhood climbed over, pouring into the yard.

Fear overwhelmed Ryan as he grabbed the house's doorknob and for a moment he couldn't decide which was worse, the idea of getting captured and brain-stung or the weird things he was sure waited for him in the house.

"Most times fear hurts you more than the thing you're afraid of," Ryan almost heard his father say, and with that he forced the door open, pulled Corrine inside behind him, slammed it shut, and bolted it.

Inside, the house was indeed dusty and overrun by spider webs, but they seemed like the kind of cobwebs found in any abandoned house. "T-This doesn't look so bad," Corrine said.

Ryan didn't have time to respond as dozens of brain-stinger spiders skittered out from holes in the floorboards, cracks in the wall and every other opening in sight.

"Never talking again," Corrine moaned in frustration. "Never."

But Ryan just stared grimly at the brain-stingers racing across the floor towards him. "Burn them," he said but nothing happened. Ryan clenched his teeth in frustration, "Come on…"

"Fireball," Ryan said, pointing a hand at the floor and a neat little sphere of fire about the size of a softball shot from the tips of his fingers and blasted at the spiders. The ball made a tiny explosion on the floor, which blew all the surrounding spiders back five feet. As soon as they hit the floor, they flipped over using their tails, and came at the two kids again.

Ryan threw fireball after fireball, brushing the bugs back, but for every one he repelled, five more skittered in to attack them from a different direction. Ryan and Corrine found themselves backed against the door they'd just entered...the same door that now shook and buckled as their brain-controlled neighbors pounded on it from the outside.

Corrine clung to his arm and let out a little whimper.

The spiders swarmed in from one side as the townspeople pounded from the other. Ryan thought once again of the webs overtaking Akashalon, and how the city's walls had formed from fire in that illusion.

"Wall of fire!" Ryan shouted, and immediately he and Corrine were surrounded by a curtain of flames, from floor to ceiling, which kept the spiders from attacking. Silently Ryan commanded the fire not to burn Corrine or the house.

Corrine smiled with relief, but Ryan dropped to his knees. "Ryan!" Corrine shouted and put a concerned hand on his shoulder.

He got back to his feet and smiled at her. "I'm OK. I just got a little dizzy," Ryan said. "I think it's the fire."

"It doesn't feel that hot. It's almost like we're protected from it," Corrine replied.

"We are," Ryan said, "but generating the fire… It's making me tired."

"Well, we're trapped here. Do you have enough for a

tunnel through it?" she said.

"I'll try," Ryan said and then commanded, "Tunnel!" The wall of fire parted to each side, making a safe passage away from the door, with the spiders trapped on both sides.

Feeling his second wind, Ryan held Corrine's hand and led her through. Without even speaking, he willed the fire to close the tunnel behind them in case the zombies outside broke through.

They followed the tunnel into the great room, where the ceiling was twice as high as the rest of the rooms in the house. The place was filthy and run down, with the splintering wooden floorboards covered in a thick layer of dust. Scattered around the room were piles of debris along with lumber, broken plaster, and window glass, all left behind by renovators that had never finished their work.

And in the far corner of the room was a sight as fearsome as it was surreal. A massive web ran from the floor all the way up to the two-story ceiling. Dark shadows obscured much of it, but Ryan could see a figure reclining at the center like a king sitting on his throne.

"Sssso, Fire Prinsssss," the shadowy person said, his voice rasping and hissing and clicking through the words. "We finally meet faissss to faissss."

Although he couldn't see the man well in the darkness, Ryan was sure that this was the same guy he and Donut has seen at the window a few days earlier.

"Who is he?" Corrine asked.

"Why don't you show yourself?" Ryan challenged the dark figure.

"Why don't you come here and take a clossssser look?" whispered the figure.

"I've got a better idea," Ryan replied. "Ball of light."

A glowing fireball appeared near the center of the room, illuminating every corner of it, and Ryan and Corrine recoiled at the terrible sight as the figure jumped down to the floor from his resting place in the web, for he seemed to be a monster more than anything else.

Although he walked on two legs and wore billowing robes that had an almost priestly quality to them, the grotesque figure was more spider than human. It had three arms on either side of its body, each one long, slender, and ending in a three-digit claw. Its head was even more terrifying, narrow and hairy, with eight eyes above a large set of pincers for its mouth, where the words hissed out.

On the outside of his robe was a strange metallic box, connected to a harness that passed over his shoulders. The device glowed, as if filled with electronics, but it looked unlike any gadget Ryan had ever seen. It had thick tubes and wiring wrapped in odd, asymmetrical patterns that made it look futuristic and clunky at the same time.

"Who are you? Are you responsible for the brain-stingers? Why have you done this to our town?" Ryan demanded.

"My name isss K'lax. Indeed, K'lax controlsss the little onesss with this," the human spider croaked as it ran a claw over the strange metal box. He poked the controls, and Ryan heard the tiny stampede of a legion of spiders skittering in the walls. K'lax poked the box again and the stampede stopped. It seemed to be a remote control.

"Why hasss K'lax done thisss?" the bug man asked. "You are the 'why,' Fire Prince. Akassshalon is the city of my people, the Arachnovar. It hasss been without a king for thousandsss of yearsss. Long has K'lax sssearched for the heir to the throne, the one who would wear the crown of fire."

"He's talking about you," Corrine whispered.

"So…what?…I'm the king of Akashalon?" Ryan asked.

"Only if you assscend the throne," K'lax clicked.

"Well if I'm your king, I command you to release my friends and family," Ryan said, hoping the quiver in his voice didn't undermine his regal authority.

K'lax cocked his head to the side. His eyes blinked in pairs, cascading down his head until all eight had opened and closed. Then he began to shake and convulse. A chilling sound escaped from his gaping mandibles, like a gagging moan from a sick person. Ryan and Corrine exchanged disgusted glances, unsure what this display from the man-spider meant.

When K'lax finally came out of his fit he said, "Boy, you misssunderstand K'lax terribly. K'lax did not ssseek you out in order to crown you."

The Arachnovar man poked the buttons of his strange controller once more and a low rumble started in the ground beneath them.

"Akassshalon is ours! We'll never cede it back to your kind!" he shouted through his pincers, "K'lax is here to kill you!" And with that, the ground began to shake. Plaster from the ceiling of the old house began to fall and dust clouded the air. K'lax just clicked and hissed, his head thrown back in apparent glee.

"Earthquake!" Corrine said and ran for a nearby window. She tried to open it, but layers of paint sealed it firmly. Just as Ryan started to follow her, the floor between them exploded from below, throwing wood and dust into the air.

As the cloud cleared, Ryan saw that a massive shape had burst up through the floor. He realized with awe and dread that this hairy thing, which was tall enough to reach from the floor to the high ceiling, was actually the segmented leg of what must have been a spider bigger than the house itself!

Ryan ran past it to Corrine, who still struggled with the window. Grabbing a hunk of concrete from the floor, he pushed her aside and threw it right through the glass. Wrapping his hand in his denim jacket, he cleared away any jagged edges that were still on the frame.

The ground shook again. The house made a low, groaning noise as its wooden frame strained under the tremors. Then another massive spider-leg burst through the floor. Ryan saw the hallway they had come through was collapsing, and the whole house was beginning to tilt.

"Go!" Ryan shouted as he boosted Corrine into the window. "I'm right behind you."

Corrine passed through the window just as the ground shook again, this time so violently that Ryan fell down. The whole floor tilted, collapsing into the basement from which the giant legs were emerging.

As Ryan slid away from the window, he looked up through the dust. Hovering above him was a spider's head so big it almost filled the room. It was a mass of thick hair with eight black eyes the size of dinner plates. A giant set of jaws lined with jagged teeth opened and closed with a horrible cracking noise.

"Behold, the Mygantuan!" K'lax raved.

"Behold…the Mygantuan!"

Suddenly the roof of the house exploded, revealing a field of stars behind the giant spider's head. It was the creature's huge scorpion-like tail, blown up to the size of a wrecking ball, that had broken through the ceiling, and now hovered above the giant spider's head.

The rumbling ground caused Ryan to slide faster and faster until he slipped off the floor altogether and fell into the basement, rolling past the Mygantuan's massive, furry underbelly.

The basement floor was also sloped downward in what Ryan imagined was a crater the same size as the one that had appeared on highway.

The realization that the big beast above him was what created that hole in the desert was the last thought Ryan had before he tumbled down into the hole, falling into complete darkness.

"...Always familiars of the Firekind..."

Chapter Eleven

Battle for Main Street

For one strange moment, Ryan felt as if the entire world was nothing but a tiny but intense ball of pain. Soon his head cleared, and he remembered what had happened. He had fallen and landed hard. That pain was just the aches in his body as he returned from unconsciousness.

Ryan held his throbbing head. He tried to open his eyes, but couldn't seem to at first. Then he realized they were already open, and he was sitting in complete darkness, at the bottom of the hole that the massive spider had made.

Ryan crawled around, probing with his hands to find his way. He wasn't sure how far he'd fallen, or if there was

even a way out. He was getting scared. To make matters worse, his hand fell on a thick, lumpy object that squirmed away when he touched it.

The moving thing startled Ryan and he fell back on the dirt floor. This is no time to be afraid, he thought. Corrine was up there with that monster bug! He extended his arm and created a small fireball in his open hand, lighting the underground space.

It was a small cave with a massive tunnel leading up and another leading down. In the light, Ryan saw what his hand had touched: all around him were Gila Monsters.

"Go away," Ryan cried out and the fireball flared brightly, but the Gilas just looked at him, blinking their wise, ancient eyes and slightly nodding their heads.

All through the cave Ryan heard a wisp of noise, like quiet, tiny voices whispering. He remembered what had happened in his bedroom, and realized it was the fire speaking to him.

"I can't understand you," Ryan said, nervously.

The whispering sound increased and words

started to form: *"Fear... familiars... Firekind... power... lend... fire..."*

"What? Speak up," Ryan said.

"...not fear them... always familiars of Firekind... lend them fire," the whispers said.

Ryan looked into the dark eyes of the closest lizard. He remembered how a Gila ate the brain-stinger in the desert. A smile crossed his lips...

* * *

K'lax sat atop the shoulders of the Mygantuan as it strode through the suburbs of Gila Flats, doggedly pursuing Corrine, who ran as fast as she could ahead of it. The Arachnovar assassin clung to the beast with six of his eight limbs.

"You will not essscape K'lax," he shouted. "You will make fine bait for the Fire Prince, ssshould we fail to find his body."

The giant spider was closing fast, and Corrine's legs

were aching, but she had to keep going. Just when she thought she couldn't run any further, Corrine reached the spot where she and Ryan had hid the scooter. She jumped on, fired the engine, and peeled away, just as a massive spider foot came down behind her.

She pushed the scooter to go as fast as it could, but it barely stayed ahead of the massive, thundering strides of the spider. Her mind raced around all the horrible events of the day, but the one thought that troubled her most was what K'lax had just said about finding Ryan's body.

"I know you're O.K., Ryan," Corrine whispered and skidded around a corner to Main Street. She hoped the bigger buildings would slow the spider down long enough for her to find a place to hide.

The Mygantuan entered Main Street and balked momentarily. Corrine thought her plan might work as the spider studied the crowded space. But it didn't hesitate long before forcing its way around the corner, its bulbous body rubbing against Smith's grocery store as it went past. The building groaned with the strain before one of its walls collapsed, allowing the spider to pass.

Corrine looked back at the chaos, encouraged that she had gained a slight lead, but when her eyes returned to the road ahead, her heart sank. A mob of her neighbors, all standing shoulder to shoulder, blocked the road, staring her down with their glazed eyes.

The scooter screeched to a halt. K'lax and his Mygantuan approached from the east. A horde of mind-slaves blocked her to the west. There were buildings on either side of her, with nowhere to run. To make matters worse, the scooter died.

"No!" she shouted and tried to kick start the scooter, but the little engine just sputtered. She tried again and again, each time whimpering in frustration. On the third try, a low but powerful rumble shook the bike and vibrated through her body. Corrine thought for a moment that she'd succeeded, but it wasn't the bike that was rumbling…it was the street itself!

The ground shook, just as it had at the Oobakka ranch. The windows of Albert's ice cream shop cracked.

Bricks fell from the roof of Thompkin's Hardware store.

Just up the road, Jones' Garage, which stood next to the spider, collapsed, creating a massive plume of sandy dust.

A giant, dark shape crawled from the dust, not on eight legs, but on four, thick, leathery limbs that ended in massive five-toed claws.

A huge head poked out of the dust. It resembled a Gila Monster's head, only it was the size of a house. Its skin was black and cracked, like cooled lava. In between the cracks, the creature glowed bright orange. Its eyes, too, looked like polished stone that swirled with fire inside.

A mighty roar issued forth from the creature's massive jaws, which were big enough to swallow several large trucks in one gulp, and hit the Mygantuan with a blast of hot breath. The big spider backpedaled, sending K'lax toppling off his perch and crashing to the cement below.

But it was what Corrine saw when the beast closed its mouth that started her heart pounding. Ryan rode atop the giant lizard, straddling its neck like a cowboy on a horse!

* * *

"OK, Magma. I hope you know what to do," Ryan said. He reached down and patted the hulking head of his giant companion. The creature's skin was so hard it felt like patting cement.

Down in the cave Ryan had listened to what the flame told him. He wasn't sure how it worked, but he agreed to lend his fire to the Gila. Ryan felt the energy coursing through his body as he relaxed and commanded the flame to go to the lizard.

The energy channeled from him to the Gila Monster, enveloping it in a column of fire. Slowly the lizard began to mutate and grow within the flame until it was large enough to tunnel through the ground.

Sitting atop Magma, as he had named the overgrown beast, Ryan found himself face to face with K'lax's terrifying spider again. The Mygantuan's eight black eyes seemed to stare blankly into Ryan's, a rainbow of color oozing over them like a layer of oil on top of a puddle of water.

Ryan gulped. Down in the cave he'd poured as much fire as he could into Magma. He'd exhausted himself doing it, but his lizard was still not as big as the giant spider.

The Mygantuan's razor-lined mandibles opened and it let out an eerie rippling noise that was half scream and half hiss. It shuffled from side to side, as if trying to outflank the lizard, but the narrow canyon formed by the buildings on Main Street confined it.

As they angled for position, Magma's head nodded

back and forth, slowly tracking the arachnid. Each time the spider lunged forward, the reptile would counter, opening its giant mouth and snapping at the spider's legs. At first it looked as though the spider, fearsome and ugly as it was, feared Ryan's new friend, but doubt crept into his mind. Something was not right.

Ryan had been staring into the swirling rainbow that covered the Mygantuan's eyes. He was half-mesmerized by it whirling colors, and so was the giant lizard. Maybe it was a whisper from the fire, or maybe it was just Ryan's intuition, but he suddenly understood that the spider was laying a trap!

They had been watching the beast's eyes, not noticing that towering high above them was the Mygantuan's wrecking-ball of a tail, poised for a strike. And strike it did, hurtling down at Ryan and his pet.

WHAM! The massive bludgeon slammed on Magma's thick head, sending the giant lizard's chin smashing into the blacktop street, which cracked under the blow. Ryan went sprawling, sliding down the reptile's

Ryan rode atop the giant lizard

shoulder onto the street.

It took him only a second to get to his feet, but that was enough time for the gigantic spider to raise its deadly tail up for another strike. Magma lay flat on the tarmac, his eyes closed.

"No! Magma!" Ryan shouted. He felt sick, unsure if the creature was still alive, and wishing he had given it more fire. He didn't have time to check on Magma, as the Mygantuan's evil eyes fixed on him again. Ryan ran, knowing he was now the target of that deadly tail.

WHAM! The spider's tail struck the street behind him, missing Ryan but shaking the ground enough to send him flying. Stars burst as he landed hard, bits of broken sidewalk bouncing off him. Ryan rolled over on his back and saw that the spider loomed over him.

A ball of fire erupted from Ryan's hand and shot towards the spider, but missed. Ryan winced as he saw that the Mygantuan's huge tail was poised to strike again and there was no time for him to get clear.

Like lightning from the sky, the spider's tail hurtled

down once more, but this time a moving wall of black and orange blocked it.

Magma was alive and fighting! Ryan's fireball wasn't meant for the spider, but was instead a spark meant to revive his reptilian friend.

Magma caught the deadly tail in its mouth and bit down hard. Sickly black juice spurted out as the Mygantuan screamed its hideous, high-pitched scream again, this time in pain. With a twist of its head, the mutant lizard tore the stinger away from the mighty tail. Just as the small Gila had done in the desert earlier, Magma threw its head back and gulped down the segment.

The spider screeched in agony and flailed its tail stub around, furious that it struck nothing. Magma advanced on the overgrown bug. The spider snapped its jaws again, hoping it could frighten what it had failed to harm. But if the thick-skinned lizard had shaken off the death strike from the tail, then it had little to fear from the spider's mouth.

Magma lunged forward with its gaping, steel-trap mouth and clamped down on two of the Mygantuan's tree-trunk legs. The spider grabbed desperately at buildings as the lizard dragged it along the street, but it was hurt badly, and its strength was fading fast.

The reptile dragged its prey to the hole it had created under Jones' Garage and pulled it down into the earth. The last thing Ryan saw was the Mygantuan's legs trying to hold on to the edge of the hole before the ground crumbled and both monsters disappeared into the darkness.

Now all Ryan had to worry about was an Arachnovar assassin and about a million brain-stingers.

"Your pet won, it appearsss, but K'lax ssstill hasss the advantage," came the clicking voice from behind Ryan. There was K'lax, perched on the thick metal pole that supported a street lamp and sign, clinging to it with four of his eight limbs.

But the sight that shattered Ryan was what that hung from the signpost, suspended over the street. It was a large cocoon of webbing that swayed back and forth. At the top of the cocoon was an opening and inside Ryan saw Corrine's eyes, her mouth covered by webs, tears streaming down her cheeks.

"Sssurrender, and K'lax will ssset her free," the man-spider taunted. "Promissse to kill you quickly."

"D-Don't worry, Corrine," Ryan said. He felt his whole body shaking.

"D-Don't w-w-worry C-c-c-c," K'lax mocked him. "Ssso unssseemly for the young prince to ssstammer in fear. Although K'lax is most fearsssome."

It was true, Ryan was afraid of K'lax. He'd used so much fire to power up Magma that he wasn't sure if he had anything left to fight with. Ryan looked up into Corrine's terrified eyes and knew he had to do something, "Burn K'lax!"

At his command, the man-spider's robes burst into flames.

Ryan's legs buckled. He knew he'd used the last of the fire. He hoped it was enough, but K'lax threw off the robes and skittered to the top of the lamp unharmed. He was naked now, except for that weird control box harnessed to his slender, mantis-like torso.

K'lax reached down from his perch and held a menacing claw against Corrine's neck. He convulsed, laughing in his weird voice as the webs muffled the girl's screams.

"Young prince knowsss not the code of fire," K'lax sneered. "You may not command it to take a life. It isss written. Now sssurrender or ssshe diesss."

Ryan tried to be strong, but there was no way he could think of to beat K'lax. He seemed to know everything while Ryan knew nothing. He was out of fire and, even if he was fully charged, it seemed he couldn't use his newfound abilities against his attacker.

"O-O.K.," Ryan said, holding his hands in the air. "You win. Just don't hurt her."

In one astonishing move, the man-spider leaped off the street post, jumping thirty feet and pouncing on the boy. Ryan was knocked flat on his back and K'lax stood over him, his six arms outstretched.

Ryan cringed in disgust as threads, like gossamer, sprayed forth from tiny digits on K'lax's elbows. He was spinning a web! Ryan tried to resist but the strands, which had seemed light and silky, turned out to be strong as steel. Soon he was covered in his own cocoon and immobilized.

K'lax crouched over the boy, his eight limbs all touching the ground like a normal spider's would. His fanged mouth opened wide, and slimy strands of drool oozed out.

"K'lax doesn't think thisss will be quick after all. It has been a long time sssince K'lax has tasssted the blood of the Firekind. K'lax meansss to sssavor it," he said. "After

K'lax is done with you, K'lax will get word to the kingdom. Your parents, your friends…even your precious Corrine…they'll all make a fine feast."

Ryan saw the control box harnessed to K'lax's body. He knew that K'lax would use it to command his brain-stingers to hold all the townspeople of Gila Flats helpless, just as he held Ryan helpless right now. Despair swirled in the pit of his stomach and rippled through his entire body. Corrine, Mom, Dad, Donut, Albert…even old Mrs. Wilkensen…they would just stand there looking sleepy until the Arachnovars had fed on them all. He had to save them.

Ryan closed his eyes and breathed deep. Even if he had used up his flame, he was still the Fire Prince. The fire was his to command, and he would not let everything end like this.

"Armor!" Ryan shouted, and in an instant he was engulfed in a sheath of hot, red flame that burned away the webs around him.

Shielding his face, K'lax tried to retreat, but Ryan

He was engulfed in a sheath of hot, red flame

reached out and grabbed the control box with his flaming hands. He held the device until it sparked and popped and its lights went dark. His flame went white-hot and the metallic box was reduced to silver slag. K'lax shrieked in pain as hot metal burned his spidery skin.

All around them, the brain-stingers that rode on the townsfolk's necks popped off and flailed on the ground, confused and disoriented now that they were cut off from the master's commands. One by one, each spider scrabbled to its tiny feet and scurried into the shadows.

Ryan stood up, a blanket of flame still pulsing over his body and faced K'lax with a defiant smile on his face.

"Curssse you, boy," K'lax said. "K'lax will kill you with claws if K'lax must."

"Burn his air away," Ryan commanded and K'lax too became engulfed in flames. The fire didn't burn him, for that was not allowed, but it consumed the air around him, leaving him with none to breathe.

"Nooooo!" K'lax gasped, scurrying away from the Fire Prince. The crowd parted as the man-spider ran past, looking like a large, eight-legged fireball.

In an eerie sight Ryan would never forget, K'lax scurried up the side of the hardware store. He ran across the rooftops, hopping from one to the next, before he reached the hole in the ground where Jones' Garage had stood. K'lax disappeared down the hole, and Ryan noticed that all the tiny brain-stingers were running for the pit as well.

Ryan walked below the cocoon that held Corrine and slowly the armor of fire around his body disappeared. "Free her," he whispered. Flames quickly disintegrated the web cocoon, but left Corrine unharmed. With a startled shriek, she dropped into Ryan's arms.

"I knew it," she said. "You are a hero."

Corrine planted a kiss on his cheek, and suddenly all the thoughts of the horrible things that had just happened vanished, and Ryan found himself giddy and lightheaded.

"I was so scared," Corrine said. "Weren't you?"

"Yeah," Ryan said, "but my Dad always says fear hurts you more than the thing you're afraid of."

Donut ambled over to the pair with a bewildered

look on his face.

"Donut, are you O.K.?" Ryan asked, not really sure of what happened to someone after a brain-stinger takes control and then lets go.

"R-Ryan? Hey, Corrine," Donut said, "What's going on? Why is everyone standing around in the street?"

Epilogue

"I think he loves you," Corrine said as she sat next to Ryan on the swing chair on the Morales' porch.

"No! He…we…we're just connected now. Like friends," Ryan said, flustered.

They both looked down at the big Gila Monster that sat on the other side of Ryan. This was Magma reduced back to his normal size, no more than thirty inches from nose to tail.

"He probably just wants his fire back," Ryan said laughing. "I think he remembers being a giant… being mighty."

Corrine held Ryan's hand as they sat under the stars.

"If he remembers, then he's the only other one," she said.

Ryan knew she was right. Some of the residents had fleeting memories of a fireball bouncing over the roofs of the town the same night that they had all found themselves standing in the middle of Main Street, but nobody recalled exactly what had happened.

Some people insisted there had been giant sinkholes where Jones' Garage and the Oobakka ranch once stood. But by the next morning, those holes had been filled in.

Everyone remembered the hole in the highway, but that too was covered over. The more observant folks noticed that there were strange scratch marks around the places where the craters had been. To the more imaginative townspeople, the markings looked as if they were made by a huge creature that had somehow pushed dirt into the hole with giant claws.

Kirby yowled and jumped into Corrine's lap. The cat had weathered the spider-invasion by hiding under the hood of Ryan's father's jeep. Now he was back to torturing old Mrs. Wilkensen, who railed against his unwelcome visits.

Things were getting back to normal everywhere. Albert replaced the windows in his ice cream shop, and was back in business within a week.

Donut haunted Albert's doorway as often as possible, his taste for good food unabated. Ryan's friend found no sign of the weird spider he had captured and held in his terrarium. There were no signs of the brain-stingers anywhere in town.

And the people worked together to rebuild Jones' Garage and to repair Smith's grocery store, and to set right the things that had been broken, even as they struggled with the unanswered questions about that mysterious night.

"Are you going to tell them?" Corrine asked, sensing what was on Ryan's mind.

"They're my parents. I have to," Ryan said. "They already know a lot of it."

He pulled the fire amulet from inside his shirt and held it so that Corrine could see it again.

"I found something new in the crystal last night," Ryan explained. "That's why I have to tell Mom and Dad. I want them to know they'll always be my true parents. And I don't want them to worry when I go away."

"Go away?" Corrine said with a frown.

"The crystal…the fire…there's a map in there," Ryan said with a smile. "We're going to Akashalon!"

Not the End…!

Heir to Fire Book Two: Zephyr Mesa

Ryan, Corinne, and Donut follow the trail
of fire to Zephyr Mesa...

...where the air elemental awaits... and the
Arachnovar assassins take their vengeance...

About the Writer

Rob Worley has been writing comics for several years, including work for Marvel Entertainment, 360ep, Narwain Publishing and Komikwerks. He has recently adapted video games and screenplays into panels and pages. Rob lives in Michigan with his two cats, Itchy and Scratchy.

About the Artist

Mike Dubisch has produced art for magazines, comics, games and toys for the last twenty years including work in *Dungeons and Dragons*, *H.P. Lovecraft's Magazine of Horror*, and Robert Jordan's *The Wheel of Time*. Mike lives in upstate New York with his wife Carolyn, his three daughters, a dog, and a million spiders in his basement.

Acknowledgements

Rob would like to thank Scott for the love of giant fire monsters, Kolleen for the big push, Tim and Chris for lending their youth, and Keith for making the connection.

Mike would like to thank Carolyn, for covering for me, and Enzo, just for nuisance value.

Creative Direction and Editor: Shannon Eric Denton
Book Design and Production: Patrick Coyle

Special thanks to John Helfers, Aron Lusen and Hope Aguilar

The publishers wish to thank Dakota, Katherine, Kristen, and Wyatt for their continued support and inspiration, and Byron Preiss for his belief in our vision.

The text type for this book is set in Baskerville.
The display type is Zigarre.
The illustrations are pen, brush, and ink.

ANOTHER GREAT BOOK FROM ACTIONOPOLIS :

The Anubis Tapestry: Between Twilights
by Bruce Zick (**Pixar**, **Disney**, **Dreamworks**)

In a race to rescue his father from the mummy's curse, Chance Henry risks succumbing to the very same fate.

Look for this book at your local bookstore, library, or comic book store. If you don't see it, ask for it by name!

More information about this and all Actionopolis books is available online: www.actionopolis.com

ISBN: 0974280380

ANOTHER GREAT BOOK FROM ACTIONOPOLIS :

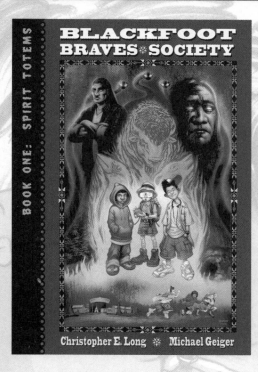

Blackfoot Braves Society: Spirit Totems

by Christopher E. Long
(*X-Men*)
and
Michael Geiger
(Sony, NBC)

Danger lurks behind the innocent adventures of summer camp as three new friends stumble upon super-natural secrets.

Look for this book at your local bookstore, library, or comic book store. If you don't see it, ask for it by name!

More information about this and all Actionopolis books is available online:
www.actionopolis.com

ISBN: 0974280399

ANOTHER GREAT BOOK FROM ACTIONOPOLIS :

The Forest King: Woodlark's Shadow
by Dan Mishkin (*Batman, Blue Devil*)
and
Tom Mandrake (*Batman, Justice League*)

A nearly forgotten legend comes horribly to life, and only one frightened boy can end its menace.

Look for this book at your local bookstore, library, or comic book store. If you don't see it, ask for it by name!

More information about this and all Actionopolis books is available online: www.actionopolis.com

ISBN: 0974280356

ANOTHER GREAT BOOK FROM ACTIONOPOLIS :

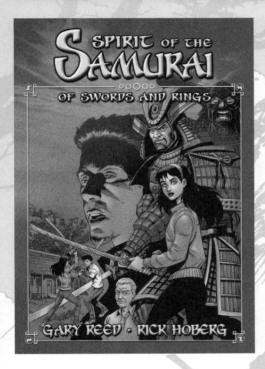

Spirit of the Samurai: Of Swords and Rings
by Gary Reed
(*Dracula,*
Frankenstein)
and
Rick Hoberg
(*Batman, Teenage*
Mutant Ninja Turtles)

When a thirteen-year-old
girl discovers the secret of
her family's ancestors, she
is drawn into an ancient
conflict still waged by the
spirits of rival samurai.

Look for this book at your local bookstore,
library, or comic book store. If you don't see it,
ask for it by name!

More information about this and all
Actionopolis books is available online:
www.actionopolis.com

ISBN: 0977880990

ANOTHER GREAT BOOK FROM ACTIONOPOLIS :

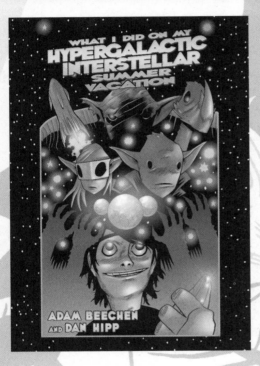

What I Did On My Hypergalactic Interstellar Summer Vacation

by Adam Beechen
(Cartoon Network & Nickelodeon)
and
Dan Hipp
(Image Comics & Tokyopop)

A restless middle-schooler finds adventure beyond his wildest dreams when he's transported across the galaxy and into the middle of an alien civil war.

Look for this book at your local bookstore, library, or comic book store. If you don't see it, ask for it by name!

More information about this and all Actionopolis books is available online: www.actionopolis.com

ISBN: 0974280364

ANOTHER GREAT BOOK FROM ACTIONOPOLIS :

Zombie Monkey Monster Jamboree
by J.J. Hart
(**Explorer, Bear Wrestler**)
and
Will Meugniot
(*Spider-Man* and *X-Men*)

While camping, a group of scouts accidentally unleash an ancient evil on the world, threatening their own lives and a nearby town. To battle the zombie monkeys will take every bit of courage and scouting skills the boys can muster--and even that might not be enough!

Look for this book at your local bookstore, library, or comic book store. If you don't see it, ask for it by name!

More information about this and all Actionopolis books is available online:
www.actionopolis.com

ISBN: 1933925078

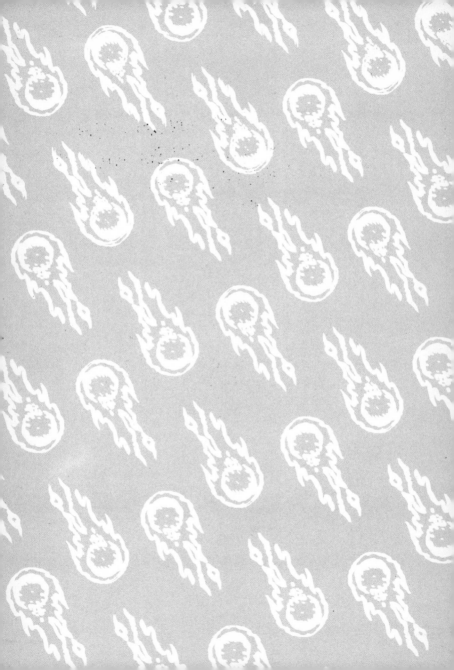